One evening, Anansi was sitting down to dinner when Turtle came to his door. Anansi knew the law of the jungle: if you have company, and you have food, you must share the food with your company.

"Come in, Turtle. You're just in time for dinner!" Anansi sighed.
Turtle sat down. "Thanks, Anansi. How are you?"

Turtle reached for a bowl of yams.
"I'm fine," answered Anansi, "but Turtle, your hands are very dirty. You know you can't sit down to dinner with dirty hands. Please go wash them before you eat."

Turtle looked sadly at his hands. They had gotten very dirty on the long walk to Anansi's house.

"Oh! You're right, Anansi. I'm sorry. I'll be right back."

Turtle slowly crawled off to wash his hands.

As soon as Turtle was out of sight, Anansi ate as fast as he could! He ate peanut soup, rice and beans and meat. *Slurp, slurp, gobble-gobble, munch-crunch, BURP!*

When Turtle got back, the bowls and plates were nearly empty. "Anansi, you've been eating all of the food!" Turtle said unhappily.

"Well, Turtle, you are very slow. I had to eat it before it got cold. But there's plenty left -- help yourself," said Anansi. "Thanks, Anansi. I'm really hungry."

Turtle reached for the bowl of rice.
"Wait!" cried Anansi. "Your hands are still dirty, Turtle!"

Turtle looked at his hands. Yes, they were dirty again, because he had crawled back to the table across Anansi's dirty, unswept floors.

"Oh! Sorry, Anansi, I'll be right back."

Turtle crept back to wash again. Then he searched through
his shell and found some nice, soft slippers to keep his hands
and feet clean.

Then he started back as fast as he could go.

But as soon as he was gone, Anansi had stuffed the rest of the food into his mouth. *Slurp, slurp, gobble-gobble, munch-crunch, BURP!*

When Turtle saw the empty table, he cried, "Anansi, you have eaten everything!" "Turtle, I could not wait any longer. The food was getting very cold. Maybe next time you come to dinner, you'll wash your hands and get to the table on time!"

Turtle nodded slowly and left with an empty tummy. As he walked, his hungry tummy growled and his hungry mind began to work.

"Hmmm! Anansi tricked me! He got me to wash my hands twice while he gobbled up all the food. It's time to teach Anansi a very important lesson!" Turtle reached home, ate his dinner, and began to plan.

The next day, Anansi found an invitation in his mailbox to go to Turtle's house for dinner.
"All right!" he cheered. "Turtle is a great cook!"

Anansi put on his best jacket and went to the edge of the pond. He saw Turtle down at the bottom of the pond, setting the table.

"I'm here, Turtle! I'm here for dinner!" he called.

"Come on down, Anansi! Your dinner is almost ready!"
answered Turtle.

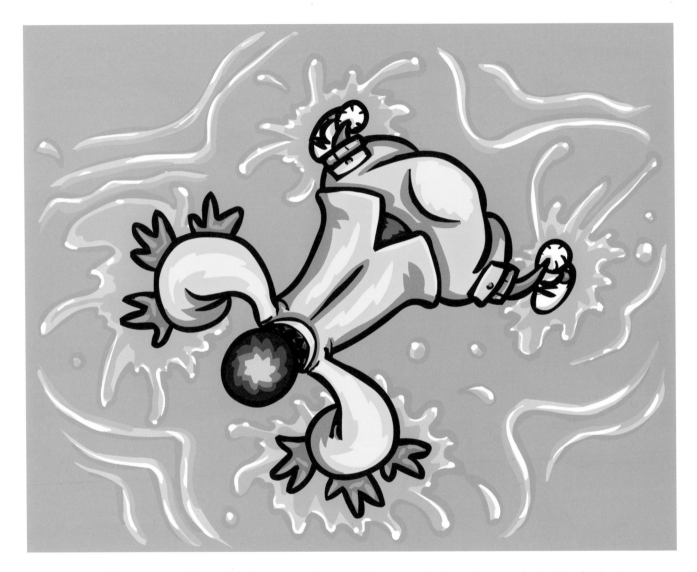

Anansi jumped into the water – *Splash!* But he didn't sink to the bottom! He just floated on the top of the water.

Anansi kicked all eight legs and bounced as hard as he could, but he could not make himself sink.
"Hurry, Anansi! Dinner is getting cold!" grinned Turtle as he watched Anansi splashing above him.

Anansi climbed out and tried again, and again, and again! *Splish, splash, splish, splash, SPLASH!* He could NOT sink to the bottom.

Anansi thought.
"Aha! I know what to do. I have big pockets in this jacket. I'll put heavy rocks in the pockets and I'll drop right down to Turtle's house!"

Anansi gathered big rocks and filled his pockets.

Then *Ker-SPLASH!* He jumped into the pond.

Glub, glub, glub! He went down, down, down to the bottom of the pond, where Turtle had set out a feast.

"This sure does look good!" said Anansi as he reached for a bowl of food.

"Wait, Anansi!" Turtle cried. "You know you can't sit down to dinner with your jacket on! Please take off your jacket."

"But, Turtle, if I take off my jacket –"
"You MUST take it off if you want to eat," said Turtle.

Anansi slowly took off his jacket and hung it on the back of his chair. He popped right back up to the top of the water!

Anansi floated and watched as Turtle ate every bite of the feast. He had plenty of time to think while he watched.

Finally he climbed out of the water and started back home. "Turtle tricked me out of a meal just like I tricked him! I guess my mama was right: What goes around, comes around!" And that's the end of that.